Red, White, and Blue Good-bye

SARAH WONES TOMP

Illustrations by
ANN BARROW

Walker & Company
New York

For Tom. Also for Zachary, Hannah, and Sam. —*S. W. T.*
For my father, my hero. —*A. B.*

First published in the United States of America in 2005 by Walker Publishing Company, Inc.

For information about permission to reproduce selections from
this book, write to Permissions, Walker & Company, 104 Fifth Avenue, New York, New York 10011.

Library of Congress Cataloging-in-Publication Data

Tomp, Sarah Wones.
Red, white, and blue good-bye / Sarah Wones Tomp ; illustrations by Ann Barrow.– 1st U.S. ed.
p. cm.
Summary: The young daughter of a Navy man does not want him to go to sea, but he points out the red flag on the mailbox,
the white clouds in the sky, and the blue ocean that will remind her of him while he is away.
ISBN 0-8027-8961-7 (hardcover) — ISBN 0-8027-8962-5 (reinforced bdg.)
[1. Fathers and daughters—Fiction. 2. Separation (Psychology)—Fiction. 3. Farewells—Fiction.] I. Barrow, Ann, ill. II. Title.

PZ7.T5979Re 2005
[E]—dc22
2004057216

The artist used watercolor and watercolor pencils on Strathmore illustration board
to create the illustrations for this book.

Book design by Victoria Allen

Visit Walker & Company's Web site at www.walkeryoungreaders.com

Printed in Hong Kong

2 4 6 8 10 9 7 5 3

Daddy is a navy man, a sailor man, a brave man.

He's my daddy too.

He's leaving soon. He'll sail away on his ship for six months,
half a year, way too many days.

Daddy's getting his stuff together. Our house is mixed up, messed up—full of piles and boxes and bags. Our house is full of Daddy getting ready to leave.

I leave first. I pack crackers and cookies and, of course, Mr. Quack. Then I run away to the shed. I climb in behind the lawn mower and the bikes and try not to look at the spiderwebs.

Mommy and Daddy call me. Mr. Quack and I sit there and listen. Sit there and wait. Sit there and miss them.

Daddy opens the shed and peeks inside. He's scolding, fussing, fuming. But then, he stops. He picks me up.

He hugs me tight and says, "Let's get out of here. Let's go make a Magnificent 'Mazing Milkshake."

We scoop, we pour,
we mix it all up.

We drink it outside. It's cold and creamy and full of strawberries. I shiver, but Daddy's arm is warm around me.

Daddy says, "Look at the mailbox. See that bright red flag on the side? The red flag goes up when you have something for me. Draw me a picture, write me a letter. Anything, anytime. Stick it in the mailbox and I'll get it.

"It'll travel all the way out to the middle of the sea, all the way round the whole world. It'll come right to me. Whenever the flag is down, I'm thinking of you. Just keep your eye on the flag."
Red flag.

Daddy has a great big giant seabag. A bag for his boots and his books and his pictures of us. Things that go with him on the ship.

I climb in. It's dark and a little dusty. My feet are smooshed, but I fit. I could go with him.

Mommy and Daddy laugh and take my picture.
But they make me get out.

Daddy and I go for a walk. We race to the end of the sidewalk. I win.

Daddy says, "Look up at that sky. See those white clouds floating along? Whenever you miss me, look for clouds and know that I'm under the very same sky. Those clouds can float between us."

Red flag, white clouds.

Daddy is looking for his big black boots with the superlong laces and supertough toes. Searching for his boondocker boots that he needs when he's working on deck. Can't go without them. Can't sail away on the ship. Just can't leave without his boots.

The boots that are under my pillow.

Daddy looks in closets and under the beds. He looks upstairs and downstairs. He looks in the shed. He looks everywhere. Almost.

His forehead is wrinkled. Daddy sits down and sighs. I climb on his lap. He looks into my eyes and says, "Do you know where my boots are?"

I have to go get the boots.
The great big boondocker boots go into the giant
seabag, right on top. His bag is full now. Too full for me.

Daddy and I go to the beach. One last time before he leaves. It's cold, but it's never too cold for us.

We run in and out of the water. Waves rush at my toes; Daddy swoops me up and out, just before they hit.

We stand in the water. Our feet sink into the wet, soupy sand. The waves try to pull us out, out to where the big ships sail.

Daddy says, "Look at the ocean. See all the blue water? I'll be sailing in this same water. I won't be so far. Just right across the ocean."

Red flag, white clouds, blue ocean.

On Daddy's last night, he tucks me in and hands me a flag.
"I have this same flag on my ship. Think of me whenever you
see red, white, and blue."

I hold the flag tight. It's the last thing I see
before I fall asleep, the first thing I see in the morning.

The big ship is waiting. One last kiss, one last hug.
Daddy swings me around one last time.

Flags are everywhere—on T-shirts, on hats, in tight sweaty palms. It's crowded. I wish Daddy would pick me up so I could see. But he's on the ship now.

There's one long blast. Engines rumble, ropes fly, the
water roars and swirls. We wave and blow kisses. The great big
ship looks smaller and smaller, way too small to hold Daddy.

We go home, to our too-quiet house. I draw pictures for Daddy. Red strawberries, white ice cream, blue cups filled with Magnificent 'Mazing Milkshakes.

Red T-shirts, white houses, blue skies. Daddy and I racing down the sidewalk.

Red swimsuits, white foam, blue waves. Daddy and I at the beach.

When my pictures are done, Mommy and I
tuck them into envelopes, seal them up with kisses,
and stick them in the mailbox. I pop up the bright
red flag.

I look at the sky. I wave to a white cloud floating by.
Floating off to my daddy, out on his ship in the deep blue sea.